Wartman

by

Michael Morpurgo

Illustrated by Joanna Carey

You do not need to read this page - just get on with the book!

First published 1998 in Great Britain by
Barrington Stoke Ltd
10 Belford Terrace, Edinburgh, EH4 3DQ
Reprinted 1998 (three times), 1999 (twice) and 2000

This edition first published 2001
Reprinted 2001

ISBN 1-902260-92-9
Previously published by Barrington Stoke Ltd under ISBN 1-902260-05-8

Printed by Polestar AUP Aberdeen Ltd

MEET THE AUTHOR - MICHAEL MORPURGO

What is your favourite animal?
Elephant
What is your favourite boy's name?
George
What is your favourite girl's name?
Eleanor
What is your favourite food?
Prawns
What is your favourite music?
'Spem in Alium' by Thomas Tallis
What is your favourite hobby?
Writing

MEET THE ILLUSTRATOR - JOANNA CAREY

What is your favourite animal?
My cat, Alfie
What is your favourite boy's name?
I have three favourites - Joseph, Felix and Daniel
What is your favourite girl's name?
Amy
What is your favourite food?
Smoked salmon
What is your favourite music?
Bach piano music
What is your favourite hobby?
Making things out of things

Contents

Chapter One

I'm telling you, it would have been a lot better if I'd broken a leg playing football.

I'd have had a plaster leg that everyone could sign. It would have been better still, if I'd been ill and had to go off to hospital. Then everyone would have sent me cards and flowers and grapes.

But I didn't break a leg and I didn't go to hospital. I got a lousy wart instead.

Typical.

I'm called Dilly, Dilly Watson. (It's Billy really, but my big brother, Jim - he's five years older

than me - called me Dilly when he was little, and it just stuck. I've been Dilly ever since.)

I was born wart-free and stayed that way for nearly nine years. My class teacher, Miss Erikson, described me to my mother at a parents' evening, when she thought I wasn't listening,

'Dilly's such a happy, smiley sort of a boy.'

And that's just what I used to be, but then things went wrong, badly wrong.

Only last term I was on top of the world. I was centre-forward in the school football team. And in the school election I was chosen as Member of Parliament. I promised them everything if they'd vote for me - a swimming pool, free sweets, a Coca-Cola fountain in the playground, an end to all lessons, and holidays whenever the sun was shining. They didn't believe a word of course, but they still voted for me - well, most of them did. Penny Prosser and her crowd didn't, but she's never liked me

anyway. Do you know what she said once? She said that football's stupid, and that Gigsy was rubbish.

I've never forgiven her for that, never. I mean, she can say what she likes about football, but to say that about Ryan Giggs! Anyway, besides Penny Prosser and her lot (and they didn't matter) everyone thought I was just about 'the bee's knees', if you know what I mean. Mr Popularity, that was me. I was top dog, King of the Castle - and Member of Parliament for Granard Primary School. *And* I was Miss Erikson's favourite too. I could tell from the way she smiled at me. But all that was last term, a long time ago - B.W. - Before the Wart.

Chapter Two

A wart comes up on you slowly. It creeps
up on you without you knowing. I had this little
pimple on my knee. It was just a tiny round
pimple. It didn't itch either, so I didn't take
much notice, not at first. Then I began to see it
every night in the bath. It didn't wash off either,
and it was always there the next night too.
Even so it still didn't really bother me. I mean,
everyone has pimples, don't they? Even Miss
Erikson has one, on her arm, just above
her watch. I've seen it.

Anyway, one evening I was sitting on the
sofa with my big brother Jim. We were just
watching television.

'You shouldn't do that, Dilly,' Mum said
to me.

'Do what?'

'You're picking at it. You shouldn't pick at it.
You'll get them all over your hands if you're not
careful.'

'What d'you mean?'

'Warts, Dilly,' she said.

'Warts! I haven't got warts!'

'Only one at the moment, Dilly,' she said.
'But you go on fiddling with it and it'll get
bigger. They spread you know.'

'Like mushrooms, silly Dilly,' said Jim. 'You
should only pick them first thing in the
morning. That's what I heard. Who's a Silly Dilly
then?'

Jim could be a real pain sometimes. Luckily for me Mum thought so too, and so did Dad.

'You are *disgusting*, Jim,' said Mum. And she sent him out to get some shoes on.

Jim was always slouching about the house in his bare feet - Mum couldn't stand that. And he was always playing his music too loud upstairs - Dad really hated that. I was definitely the goody-two-shoes in the family, and I liked it that way.

'Don't take any notice of him, Dilly,' Mum said when he'd gone out.

'It's not really a wart, is it?' I asked her.

Mum sat down beside me on the sofa and looked at it more closely. 'Looks like it to me, Dilly. I've been noticing it for a few weeks now. But it'll be all right. It'll go away on its own, but only if you *leave it alone.*'

Jim was singing as he went upstairs, loudly, deliberately loudly, so that we could hear. 'Who's got a wart, Dilly, Dilly? ... Who's got a wart ... ?'

'Jim!' Mum shouted, and he shut up.

I was bending over, anxiously inspecting my knee as I often did.

'What if it doesn't, Mum?' I asked.

'Doesn't what, dear?'

'Doesn't go away.'

'It will, Dilly. They always do - in the end. Just forget about it.'

Jim started up again upstairs. 'Who's got a wart, Dilly, Dilly? Who's got a wart ... ?'

And Mum went up to sort him out.

After that I tried all I could not to touch it, not to think about it. But it still didn't go away and worse, I could see it was definitely getting bigger and bigger. No matter how I looked at it, my pimple was not a pimple any more. It was a wart, and it was growing harder and whiter and more knobbly every day. Sooner or later

I knew someone was going to notice it at school - probably that Penny Prosser, knowing my luck. I couldn't let that happen.

So here's what I did. I bought a large packet of Elastoplast, with my own pocket money too. Cover it up, I thought, and no one would see it and, you never know, Mum might be right after all, it might just go away. But it didn't.

Chapter Three

It was summer, and I was in shorts. I asked and I asked, but Mum wouldn't let me wear my jeans.

'Let your legs breathe a bit,' she said.

'Legs don't breathe,' I said. But she wouldn't listen.

So each day after I left the house for school, I'd dart into the alleyway opposite the house, hide behind a tree, whip out a plaster and cover up my wart. Every afternoon, on the way back from school, I'd stop there and take it off just

before I got home. Every time, just before I ripped it off, I'd hope hard that my wart would be gone, squeezing my eyes tight. But when I opened my eyes it was still there, bigger and harder and knobblier than ever. Still, at least the trick had worked. At school no one knew about my wart, not yet anyway.

At home though, things were not good. Jim kept on and on about my wart, never letting me forget it. He invented a new name for me.

'Well,' he said one day, 'and how's Wartman today? Hey, Wartman, you could be in the movies. I can see you now, up in lights down at the cinema, *Dilly the Wartman - knobbly enough and nasty enough to frighten even Alien to death.*'

I had to do something, didn't I? I threw the dog bowl. It was the nearest thing I could lay my hands on. Jim ducked and the bowl sailed over his head, out through the kitchen door and into the sitting room. The next moment Dad came storming in, Mum right behind him.

'Who threw that?' he said.

He was not at all pleased, and neither was Mum. Jim shrugged his shoulders and grinned innocently.

'Not me,' he said.

I could have kicked him.

'Dilly!' said Mum. 'What's come over you? What's the matter with you?'

'He called me Wartman, Mum. He keeps on at me.'

'Sticks and stones may break my bones, Dilly,' Dad said, 'but names will never hurt me.

Silly Dilly, Wartman - what does it matter what he calls you - what's the difference?'

But there *was* a difference. Mum knew there was too, but she didn't say anything. From then on it was downhill for me all the way, with Jim enjoying every shove.

Chapter Four

First thing he'd say to me in the morning would be, 'Out of the bathroom, Wartman.' And then at breakfast, 'Pass the milk, Wartman.'

He'd even call me Wartman in front of his friends when they came to the house. Mum looked daggers at him, but she never stopped him. Things were going from bad to worse.

I was sitting on my bed one night. Jim's music was pounding and thumping away next door, as usual. I was just looking at my wart, worrying about it, when Jim came in.

'Love,' he said, clicking his fingers to the music. 'It's the only thing, Wartman.'

'What?'

'You've got to learn to love it, Wartman,' he said.

I threw a slipper at him, but it missed.

It sounded silly, I knew that. Everything Jim said sounded silly, but I was thinking about it in bed that night, and it began to make a little sense. I mean, I knew I couldn't love my wart, but I also knew now that it wasn't going to disappear the next day or the day after that. So I was going to have to live with it. I decided a name could help.

So I called it 'George'. Every day after that, when I covered him with plaster in the alleyway, I'd whisper, 'G'night, George.' And when I took it off just before I got home, I'd say something like, 'Oh, hello, George. You still there?'

And he always was, as immovable as a limpet on a rock face.

But at school there was trouble, real trouble. After all, I'd been wearing a plaster on my knee for months now, and people were beginning to ask questions. I'd told everyone it was a cut, that I'd fallen off my bike at the bottom of Berry Hill. I'd gone into how the blood had gushed out onto the road, and how they'd had to rush me into hospital. I'd had four stitches - no anaesthetic either. It was a good story, and I was proud of it.

It was in P.E. one day when Miss Erikson asked me,

'Aren't they out yet, Dilly?'

'What, Miss?'

'Those stitches. In your knee.'

'Oh ... them. Yes, Miss. Last week, Miss. Doctor pulled them out.'

'How many did you say there were?' She was suspicious I could tell.

'Er ... three ... no, four, Miss. That's right, four.'

I tell you, it wasn't easy getting my story right each time, down to the last detail. Sooner or later I was going to be found out. Sooner or later my 'cut' would have to 'heal'. Somehow that plaster would have to come off. Well, the plaster did come off, but not how I'd planned it, not how I'd planned it at all.

Chapter Five

It was Wednesday afternoon playtime. A few
of us were kicking a ball around in the
playground - the field was too wet to go on.
I was doing my Gigsy style dribbling as well as
I ever had. I was flying past Darren, who could
only stand and gape at me. I was weaving
around Tom and Barry, who were already
blaming each other for the goal I hadn't yet
scored, when suddenly there was Penny Prosser,
just standing there, right in my way, right in
the middle of our game. So I went to dribble
around her towards the goal. And do you know

what she did? She stuck her foot out and tripped me!

Down I went, rolling over and over until I ended up in a heap in the goalmouth. My knees, my elbows, my nose - everything was stinging. And my head was spinning. I looked up. Miss Erikson was bending over me. She was a bit of a blur at first.

'You all right. Dilly?' she asked.

I was clutching my knee, and moaning and groaning. That was when I discovered the plaster had gone. Instead, there was a sticky, gritty graze under my hand. A crowd was gathering, staring down at me, pushing, shoving for the best place.

It was a disaster, a real disaster. I mean, I'd missed the goal for a start and my knees and my elbows and my nose burned and throbbed.

And worst of all my wart was about to be discovered. I was about to be found out.

'Let's take a look, shall we, Dilly?' said Miss Erikson. She was crouching down beside me. Her hand was cool on my leg. 'I hope it hasn't opened up that cut of yours.'

She knew! I could tell from her voice. Somehow she'd known all along.

I clutched my knee tighter still and groaned in agony. I wasn't pretending exactly, just making the most of it. Anything, I thought, anything to delay the dreadful moment when I knew I'd have to take my hand away.

'She tripped me, Miss,' I whined. 'That Penny, she tripped me. And she wasn't even in our game. It was on purpose, Miss. She did it on purpose. I know she did.'

'I never,' Penny protested. 'He just ran into me, that's all. Honest, Miss.'

Miss Erikson ignored her. She was trying to prize my fingers away, but I wouldn't let her. George was there under the palm of my hand - I could feel him - and there was blood trickling through my fingers.

'Come on, Dilly,' she said. 'I've got to see it before I know how bad it is, haven't I?'

Everyone was watching, waiting. There was nothing more I could do. I had to let her take away my hand.

There was George, naked for all the world to see, with a great black plaster mark on either side of him. And just to one side of him was a dirty red gash, so long and so wide that it looked as if it was laughing at me.

'Oooh!' said someone.

'Nasty,' said someone else.

And then just what I'd been dreading.

'Look, Miss, he's got a great big wart on his knee. And he's been covering it up with that plaster. You can see.'

It was Penny Prosser, of course. It had to be.

'I thought you fell off a bicycle,' said someone.

'Four stitches you told us,' said someone else.

'Look, Miss.' It was Penny Prosser again. She was holding up the plaster between finger and thumb. 'Yuk! Look what I found. Yuk!'

It was the worst moment of my life, and that's the honest truth. George had never looked so big and so knobbly as he looked at that moment. They were all sniggering at me now. I was sitting there, snivelling. I just couldn't stop myself.

It was Miss Erikson who saved me. She sent them all in and took me into the staffroom and sat me down.

'It's just a graze. You'll be fine, Dilly,' she said, fetching some water and cotton wool. 'I'll just clean you up a bit.'

Then she was kneeling down in front of me and dabbing my knee gently. It was warm and wet, and the drips tickled as they ran down my leg into my sock. I was still trying to stop myself from snivelling but it kept coming in hiccups, tugging at my stomach.

'Do you know, Dilly?' she was saying. 'Do you know, I had two of them, two warts just like yours, only bigger?' I thought she was just being kind. 'No, honestly Dilly,' she went on. 'I had them a long time ago, just after I came to this school. They've gone now, gone completely.'

'But how?' I asked. 'Mum said George would go, but he hasn't.'

'George?' she said.

So I introduced her to George and she smiled at me. She wasn't laughing at me, just smiling. Miss Erikson has the whitest teeth I've ever

seen. Somehow I wasn't snivelling any more. She stopped her dabbing and held up her hand.

'I had one on this finger, and one on my thumb, here. One day they just disappeared completely - as if they'd never been there.'

It was true. There was nothing there. There wasn't a mark. She leaned closer.

'And I'll tell you something else, Dilly. I didn't give them names, but I did put a plaster on, to cover them up. So no one would notice.'

'Just like me then?'

'That's right,' she said, dabbing on some antiseptic. 'This will sting a bit, I'm afraid.'

She was right. It did sting, but I didn't mind.

'You're a brave boy, Dilly,' she went on, as she strapped on a big pink plaster over my knee.

'But how, Miss? How did they go? How did you get rid of them?'

'Ah well, that's a strange story,' she said. Then she looked at her watch. 'If I told you, you wouldn't believe me. I wonder ... I wonder ... I've got an idea, Dilly. School will be over in about half an hour. I'm going to phone your Mum and tell her I'll be bringing you home myself. As soon as school's over, go and sit in my car and wait for me. We're going on a little trip.'

'Where to? Where are we going?' I asked.

'You'll see, Dilly. You'll see.'

It wasn't easy walking into that classroom, I can tell you. Penny Prosser started her sniggering again, but Miss Erikson soon shut her up, with one flash of her eyes. No one else bothered me after that.

We always have storytime last lesson. Today Miss Erikson was reading us a story about a

sultan and a cockerel. But I just could not concentrate on sultans and cockerels. All the time I was wondering where Miss Erikson was going to take me after school, and how on earth she had managed to get rid of her warts. Before I knew it the bell rang for the end of school.

Chapter Six

I waited in Miss Erikson's car, just as she had told me to. I looked down at George. I rubbed away the last of the black plaster marks, so that by the time Miss Erikson came out he looked unframed, and a bit lonely, beside the bright pink of the new plaster.

'He's still there, is he?' said Miss Erikson, getting into the car beside me. 'I phoned your Mum. She says it's all right. Put your seat belt on, Dilly.'

'Where are we going, Miss?' I asked. 'Is it far?'

'It's not that far,' she said. 'I'm going to take you to see someone, someone who might help. He's a nice man, you'll see. He may not say very much. And he may not hear very much either. He's old and he's a bit deaf too. But he can cure warts. He cured mine anyway. He just magicked them away.'

'How, Miss?'

'I don't know, Dilly. No one knows. Doesn't really matter, does it?'

'You mean he's a sort of witch doctor?'

'Sort of,' said Miss Erikson.

'Does it hurt, Miss?'

She laughed. 'Of course not. I didn't feel a thing. Promise.' And she patted my hand. 'Don't worry, Dilly.'

But I did. I never stopped asking her questions the whole way. We drove into a sleepy-looking village and stopped by the duck pond. There was a small cottage on the far side of it, and flower pots all around it, up the front path, on the window sills, everywhere.

'That's his place, she said. 'Mr Ben. Everyone just calls him Mr Ben. Ready?'

'Ready,' I said.

Miss Erikson had to rap the knocker again and again before he came. The door opened very slowly.

'It's me, Mr Ben.' Miss Erikson was speaking louder than usual. The old man looked a bit puzzled. 'I phoned, remember?' she went on. 'You cured my warts.'

He was the oldest man I'd ever seen in all my life. I never thought people could be that old.

He had silver-white wispy hair, and glasses that sat on the end of his nose. There were holes in the toes of his slippers.

'Oh yes, come in my dear,' he said. 'I've been expecting you.'

We followed him in as he shuffled down a passageway and into a little room at the back. Everything smelt musty, and it looked musty too. All the walls were brown, the furniture too. He sat down in a battered, old, leather chair, and eyed me steadily.

'This is the boy?' said Mr Ben. 'Are you the boy?'

'Dilly,' said Miss Erikson loudly, taking me by the elbow. 'This is Dilly.'

'Hello, Billy,' he said, and Miss Erikson and I looked at each other. There wasn't much point in correcting him. Besides, I thought, I *was* Billy.

He'd got my name *right*. He was the first person to get it right in nine years.

'It's on his knee, Mr Ben,' Miss Erikson went on, pointing to my knee. 'He's got a wart on his knee.'

Mr Ben beckoned me closer. Then he leaned forward to look. He sucked in air through his teeth, and shook his head slowly.

'Oooh, nasty one,' he said. 'They're devils, these warts, you know. Now, a common cold, I can cure him easy as pie. But warts, they're always difficult little devils. But I'll see what I can do, shall I? Come a little closer, Billy, there's a good boy. I've got to get a good, long look at him.'

So I went close, really close. His eyes were almost touching my knee by this time. I heard him take a deep breath, and then another and another. He was holding my knee now, gripping it hard with both hands.

There was silence all around us, complete silence. It seemed as if everyone in the room had stopped breathing. No one moved.

Then George began to tickle. I wanted to scratch him, but somehow I didn't dare move. It was like having your photograph taken. The tickle was turning into a tingle. I glanced down at George expecting him to have gone. But he was still there.

Mr Ben sat back in his chair, took out a handkerchief and wiped his eyes.

'All done, Billy,' he said.

'Thanks.'

I didn't know what else to say.

'Oh, don't thank me, Billy,' chuckled Mr Ben. 'I haven't done much, honestly I haven't. You can't do away with a wart, you know. It's not possible. All I do is send him off to feed on someone else, whoever he likes. It's the best I can do.'

It was a chilling thought, a thought I couldn't get out of my head all the way home.

*****

A week later George simply vanished,
disappeared, wasn't there any more.

And a week after that Penny Prosser got
a wart on her finger. She says she caught it off
me but then she would say that, wouldn't she? I
know different, don't I?

And a week after that my big brother Jim
got a wart on his thumb.

Mum says she doesn't believe in Mr Ben
and all his 'mumbo jumbo', as she calls it.
She still thinks Jim must have been using
my towel, but I know better, and so does Miss
Erikson.

And Mr Ben put more than my wart right.
He put my name right too. He called me Billy.
I know it was by mistake, but I liked it. I liked it
a lot, so I decided that from then on I would
always be called Billy.

I told everyone.

No one calls me Dilly any more, except Jim.
From time to time he still calls me 'Silly Dilly'.
But that's all right, I just call him 'Wartman'
right back.

Who is Barrington Stoke?

Barrington Stoke was a famous and much-loved story-teller. He travelled from village to village carrying a lantern to light his way. He arrived as it grew dark and when the young boys and girls of the village saw the glow of his lantern, they hurried to the central meeting place. They were full of excitement and expectation, for his stories were always wonderful.

Then Barrington Stoke set down his lantern. In the flickering light the listeners were enthralled by his tales of adventure, horror and mystery. He knew exactly what they liked best and he loved telling a good story. And another. And then another. When the lantern burned low and dawn was nearly breaking, he slipped away. He was gone by morning, only to appear the next day in some other village to tell the next story.

If you loved this story,
why don't you read . . .

Who's A Big Bully Then?

by Michael Morpurgo

How would you feel if you beat the
school bully in a race? And he then
wanted a fight? How would you cope?
Find out what happens to Darren in
front of all his friends.

You can order this book directly from Macmillan
Distribution Ltd, Brunel Road, Houndmills, Basingstoke,
Hampshire RG21 6XS   Tel: 01256 302699